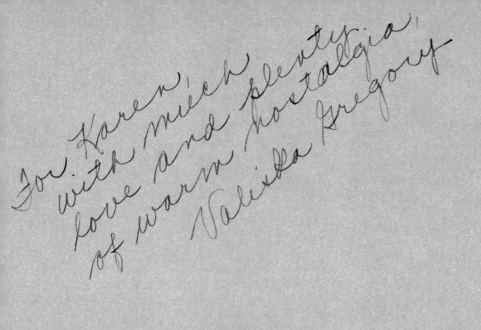

For Karen,
with much
love and plenty,
of warm nostalgia,
Valiska Gregory

Mr. Poggle and Scamp
lived together
in a comfy house
in the middle
of the deep green woods.

In the bedroom
there were two beds.
At the table
there were two chairs.
And by the fireside
there were eight paws
with brown toasty toes.

Every day
was different,
and every day
was the same.

Every morning
the sun would open
his orange eye.
And every night
the sky would tuck
her dark blue blanket
over his nose.
But what happened
in between made
all the difference.

A Mr. Poggle and Scamp Book

The Oatmeal Cookie Giant

by Valiska Gregory
pictures by Jeni Bassett

Four Winds Press
New York

For Bob and Don, the best of brothers—V.G.

For Bobby Weil—J.B.

LUCAS EVANS BOOKS

Text copyright © 1987 by Valiska Gregory
Illustrations copyright © 1987 by Jeni Bassett
All rights reserved. No part of this book may be reproduced or transmitted
in any form or by any means, electronic or mechanical, including photocopying,
recording, or by any information storage and retrieval system, without permission
in writing from the Publisher.
Four Winds Press
Macmillan Publishing Company
866 Third Avenue, New York, NY 10022
Collier Macmillan Canada, Inc.
Printed and bound by South China Printing Company, Hong Kong
First American Edition
10 9 8 7 6 5 4 3 2 1
The text of this book is set in 14 pt. Goudy Old Style.
The illustrations are rendered in pen-and-ink and watercolor wash.

Library of Congress Cataloging-in-Publication Data
Gregory, Valiska.   The Oatmeal Cookie Giant. (A Mr. Poggle and Scamp book)
Summary: Young Scamp does not expect to enjoy his visit to his stodgy old uncle,
until Uncle Thorny begins to reminisce about his own youth.
[1. Uncles—Fiction. 2. Old age—Fiction. 3. Dogs—Fiction] I. Bassett, Jeni, ill.
II. Title. III. Series: Gregory, Valiska. Mr. Poggle and Scamp book.
PZ7.G86240a 1987   [E]   87-191
ISBN 0-02-738070-X   ISBN 0-02-738080-7 (pbk.)

"Today," said Mr. Poggle, "we will visit Great-Uncle Thorny."
Scamp frowned.

"But I don't want to visit
Great-Uncle Thorny," he said. "He
has no toys and he always says
no rocking in the rocking chair.
Besides," Scamp said, "his house
smells like rotten grapefruit."

"Well now," said Mr. Poggle, "we will have to see about that. Did you know about Uncle Thorny's clock that strikes thirteen, or about the Oatmeal Cookie Giant?"

Scamp's eyes opened wide. "But
I never saw those things before."
Mr. Poggle smiled. "That's because
you did not look for fun before."

Great-Uncle Thorny sat with a
quilt tucked over his knees.
He looked at Scamp. "No rocking
in the rocking chair," he said.
"And don't eat too much or you
might throw up."
Scamp rolled his eyes up to the ceiling.

"Uncle Thorny," said
Mr. Poggle, "do you remember
when you were little and rocked
so hard you fell on your head?"

Scamp tried to picture Uncle
Thorny without any wrinkles,
falling on his head.
"And do you remember," said Mr. Poggle,
"the Oatmeal Cookie Giant?"
Great-Uncle Thorny laughed.

"Yes, of course," he said.
His voice crackled like fire.
"I didn't like to go to Great-Aunt Mary's
house," he said, "because there wasn't
much to do. Besides, her house
smelled like rotten grapefruit."
Scamp gave Mr. Poggle a quick look.

Uncle Thorny smiled. "But I *did* like Aunt Mary's oatmeal cookies," he said. His brown eyes glittered and danced as he talked.

"Well sir," he said, "one day I ate
every single cookie on the plate."
He and Scamp pretended
to gobble up all the cookies.
"And *then*," said Great-Uncle Thorny,
"in walked Great-Aunt Mary."
"Oh no," said Scamp.
"Oh yes," said Uncle Thorny.
"Well sir, I had to think fast.

"'Aunt Mary,' I said, 'you will
never guess who ate the cookies.'
'You are probably right,'
she said, 'but tell me anyway.'
'I was just sitting here all by
myself,' I said, 'when in walked

"'the Oatmeal Cookie Giant himself!

"'He was as tall as a tree and as
strong as steel. And he said
if I didn't give him those
cookies he would probably
gobble up the whole house.'

"Great-Aunt Mary stood there like
a statue, cold as ice. She said,
'Are you telling me a story?'
Well sir, I had to think
pretty hard about that."

"What did you say?" asked Scamp.
Uncle Thorny's eyes crinkled.
"I said that the story I told
was a lot more exciting than the
story that really happened."
"That was smart," said Scamp.

"Aunt Mary thought so too," said
Great-Uncle Thorny. "But next
time, she said, I should tell her
which story really happened
and which story I made up."

"And she wasn't mad about
the cookies?" asked Scamp.
"No," said Great-Uncle Thorny,
"but she did give me some
tea to settle my stomach
so I wouldn't throw up."

Scamp thought a minute.
"Sometimes," he said,
"people can surprise you."
Mr. Poggle smiled. "It is
time to go home," he said.

"But what about the clock?" asked Scamp.
Great-Uncle Thorny narrowed his eyes.
"Well sir," he said, "maybe you will
just have to come and visit me again."
Scamp narrowed his eyes too.
"Well sir," he said,
"I think that would be fun."